student · secret agent · princess

#4 Thunderstruck

Text by Stephanie Peters
Created by Larry Schwarz

Visit Princess Natasha every day at
www.princessnatasha.com.

Watch Princess Natasha on CARTOON NETWORK™
and anytime online on the KOL® service at
KW: Princess Natasha.

LITTLE, BROWN & COMPANY
LB kids™
NEW YORK BOSTON
lb-kids.com

Little, Brown and Company

Hachette Book Group USA
1271 Avenue of the Americas, New York, NY 10020
Visit our Web site at www.lb-kids.com

LB kids is an imprint of Little, Brown and Company Books for Young Readers,
a division of Hachette Book Group USA.
The logo design and name, LB kids, are trademarks of Hachette Book Group USA.

First Edition: October 2006

The characters and events portrayed in this book are fictitious. Any similarity to real
persons, living or dead, is coincidental and not intended by the author.

Based on the KOL® cartoon created by Animation Collective, Inc.

Library of Congress Cataloging-in-Publication Data

Peters, Stephanie True, 1965-
  Thunderstruck / text by Stephanie Peters ; created by Larry Schwarz ; [illustrations by
Animation Collective].
    p. cm.— (Princess Natasha ; #4)
"Based on the KOL cartoon created by Animation Collective."
  ISBN-13: 978-0-316-15508-3 (trade pbk.)
  ISBN-10: 0-316-15508-X (trade pbk.)
  I. Schwarz, Laurence. II. Animation Collective. III. Title. IV. Series: Peters, Stephanie
True, 1965- Princess Natasha ; #4.
PZ7.P441833Thu 2006
[Fic]—dc22
                                        2005033046

10 9 8 7 6 5 4 3 2 1

COM-MO

Printed in the United States of America

A Brief Zoravian History

Deep in the Carpathian Mountains lies the ancient kingdom of Zoravia. Usually, the people of this country live in peace and harmony. But there are times when darkness falls across this fair land—a darkness known as Lubek.

Fifteen years earlier, Lubek inherited control of Zoravia. But the people had long despised Lubek. They voted him off the throne and elected his brother, Carl, in his place.

Lubek fled to America and began scheming against his former homeland. For years, his exact whereabouts remained a mystery. Then Zoravian Intelligence discovered his secret identity. By day, Lubek works as a high school principal and science teacher in a small town in Illinois called . . . Zoravia.

Once known as Fountain Park, the town changed its name in honor of King Carl, Queen Lena, and their fourteen-year-old daughter, Princess Natasha. Natasha had never met her evil uncle, but she had spent her life preparing to defeat him.

And now, she'll have her chance. Trained as a secret agent, Natasha has come to Illinois, where she poses as an exchange student at Fountain Park High. No one—not her host family, her friend Maya, or her fellow students—can ever know her true identity. If Lubek ever found out who she was, it would be the end of Natasha—and her beloved Zoravia.

Chapter One

A Rustle in the Night

Natasha—princess, foreign exchange student, and undercover secret agent—sat bolt upright in bed. Something was rustling in her closet.

As quietly as she could, she slipped from under the covers and tiptoed across the room. The rustling stopped just as she reached the closet door.

She froze. *Whatever was in there must have heard me*

coming, she thought.

Then the noise started up again. She waited a beat then slowly moved her hand to the knob and eased the door open a crack.

The rustling stopped. Once again, Natasha stood stock-still and, once again, the rustling began. She pushed the door open and reached inside.

Her fingers brushed something shaggy.

"Eep!" She jerked her hand back with a squeak of alarm and waited for the "something" to jump out at her. To her great relief, nothing did. Cautiously, she reached in again, pulled the cord for the overhead light, and peered inside.

A ghastly human head with bushy black hair and buck teeth stared up at her through eyeless sockets.

This time, she didn't squeak. She kicked the hideous face hard. To her horror, her foot sank deep into the nose and the whole head caved in. She slammed the  door quickly. Her heart hammered with fear, nearly—but not quite—drowning out the sound of rustling.

Okay, she thought, *whatever that thing is, it isn't coming after me. So I guess I'll have to go after it!*

She put her hand on the knob again, took a few deep breaths, and yanked the door open. The caved-in head was still there. But this time, she looked at it more closely—and sagged against the door with a shaky laugh. It was just a rubber monster mask!

She nudged it with her toe. The grotesque

head flopped over. Underneath it was a note. She picked it up and read it.

Roses are red,
  Violets are blue,
  If you're reading
  this note,
  I bet we scared you!

The note was signed by KC and Greg, the sons of her host parents, the O'Briens. Natasha scowled, crumpled up the paper, kicked the mask into a far corner of the closet, and started plotting her revenge against the O'Brien brothers.

The rustling started again.

Her eyes slid to her backpack. It was shaking.

Her mouth turned dry. *Something's in there. And it wants to get out.*

She swallowed hard and then hooked a finger

through a shoulder strap. Lifted the pack out of the closet. Pulled the zipper open one tooth at a time. And waited.

The pack stopped quivering. She risked a peek inside. Once again, relief flooded her body. The thing trembling inside her backpack was her Booferberry! *It's on vibrate mode!* she realized, remembering how she'd switched the device from "ring" to "silent" before school that day. Then she realized

something else. If her Booferberry was vibrating, it was because her father, King Carl, was trying to contact her! She pushed a button to receive the incoming message. King Carl's handsome face appeared on the screen.

"I'd about given up on you, Natasha," he said

with a smile.

"Sorry, Dad! Little Booferberry snafu, that's all." She sat down at her desk. "Let me guess: Lubek's causing trouble again, right?"

The king's smile faded. "Reports indicate that your uncle is searching for some new technology to steal and use against Zoravia." He sighed heavily. "Unfortunately, we have no idea where he's looking or what he's looking for."

"Hmmm." Natasha drummed her fingers on the desktop. Her pinky touched a paper on her desk. She picked the paper up and scanned it quickly.

"Hold on, Dad, listen to this! 'Interested in the gadgets of the future? Then sign up with Mr. Lubek for the overnight field trip to the Fountain Park Science and Technology Museum.'" She put the paper down. "Do you think Lubek set up this trip so he can see if the museum has something worth stealing?"

"Robbing a museum is definitely something he would do," the king replied grimly. "And as it is an overnight—"

"—he'd already be inside and could make his move once everybody is asleep!" Natasha finished for him.

"You know what this means, Natasha?"

She nodded. "It means I'm going on a field trip!"

Chapter Two

Lights Out

After dinner Saturday night, Natasha joined several other students outside the Fountain Park Science and Technology Museum for the field trip.

"Hey, girlfriend!" Maya, Natasha's best friend, waved to her from beside a pile of sleeping bags.

"Hey, girlfriend!" Greg O'Brien, handsome as ever, waved to Kelly, his girlfriend. Kelly had a pretty face, killer clothes, and a head of

bright yellow hair. As far as Natasha could tell, that was the only bright thing about her.

"Yoo-hoo, uh, I mean, hey, girlfriend!" sang a short, red-haired figure with thick, round glasses. It was Oleg Boynski, Natasha's Zoravian spy partner. Oleg was a nice-enough guy and a top-notch undercover agent, but he was a little geeky.

"Hello, Prin—er, Natasha," Oleg said when she came over. "I am looking forward to this overnight." He lowered his voice. "And I am certain someone else is as well." He

nodded toward where Lubek was standing.

"We've got to stick close to him at all times," Natasha murmured in agreement.

"Like paste. I shall stick to him like paste!"

Natasha hid a smile. "I think you mean 'stick to him like *glue.*'"

Oleg shrugged. "I prefer paste. It tastes— that is, it *works* better."

Natasha looked at Oleg with a raised eyebrow. He cleared his throat and looked away.

Maya bounded up. "It's going to rain," she predicted.

Natasha glanced at the sky. Storm clouds had gathered overhead, turning the starry October evening gloomy and chilly. Suddenly, fat raindrops began to fall.

"Yikes! Let's go!"

Natasha, Oleg, and Maya gathered their belongings and hurried inside the museum with the others

On the way in, Natasha bumped into Kelly. "Oops, sorry!" she said.

"Yeah, right," Kelly replied. "You pushed me on purpose, because you're jealous!"

Maya appeared at Natasha's side. "Jealous? Of what?"

Kelly thrust out her arm. "Of this!"

"Your wrist?"

"No, what's *on* the wrist!"

Natasha and Maya bent over Kelly's hand. "You mean that piece of yellow string?" Maya asked.

"That's not *string*, that's *gold*! As in, gold *bracelet*! As in, given to me by my *boyfriend* to match the *necklace* he gave me. That's why you're jealous—because I have a boyfriend who gives me expensive jewelry!"

Natasha and Maya looked over at Greg. He was blowing an enormous bubble. Then the bubble popped and the gum covered his face with a sticky pink film.

Maya rolled her eyes. "Oh, yeah, we're soooo jealous. Anyway, your string's got something stuck in it."

Kelly narrowed her eyes. "That's the *diamond*!"

"You're joking." Maya grabbed Kelly's wrist and held it up to Natasha's nose. "You see a diamond there?"

 Kelly snatched her arm back, gave Maya a nasty look, and stalked off.

"Come on, Natasha," Maya said, laughing. "Let's

unload our stuff."

The two girls added their sleeping bags and overnight packs to a growing pile of gear. Maya's eyes widened when she saw the size of Natasha's backpack. "What do you have in there, your bed?"

"Oh, um, no, just a few extras I might need." Those "extras" were her spy suit, complete with utility belt and super-powered, high-tech, absolute-height-of-fashion glasses. She'd left her Booferberry at home, however, because she didn't want to risk a repeat of the rustling from the other night. She'd also left her Lubek Locator behind. Since she'd know where Lubek was at all times, she wouldn't need the small computer to find him for her.

"Think I'll scope out the place," she said. She headed to a balcony that overlooked the museum's main hall. The exhibits were usually overrun with visitors, but now it was after-hours, so the hall was empty and silent. Natasha scanned the different sections, wondering which one housed the technology Lubek was interested in.

Zap! BOOM!

A streak of lightning suddenly flared, filling the hall with brilliant light. The flash was followed by a deafening crack of thunder. Then all at once the museum was plunged into darkness.

Chapter Three

Hal and Hugh

Natasha gripped the balcony railing. *Steady,* she thought. *It's just a power outage.*

She heard voices to her left. She inched her hands along the railing, making her way toward the sounds. Suddenly, her left hand traveled over something cold and bumpy.

"Good eee-ve-ning," said a gravelly voice.

As if on cue, the lights came back on. Natasha found herself face-to-face—and hand in hand—with a ghostly white, cadaverous-looking man. She gasped and pulled away.

The man blinked his pale blue eyes and then flashed a yellow, toothy smile.

"Did I . . . frighten you?" he rasped.

She let out her breath. "No."

He leaned close to her face. "Not afraid of the dark, are you?"

At his words, Natasha sucked in her breath again—but not because she was frightened. *Who is this guy and what's he been eating, garlic and salami?* she thought, grimacing.

"I am Hal, your tour guide. And don't worry," he added, "the backup generator has powered up now. It will keep the lights on. Shall we join the others?"

Hal led her to where the rest of the class was gathered. When the students had quieted down, Hal introduced himself. Then he pointed a bony finger at a frizzy-haired man wearing a uniform. "This is Hugh, chief of museum security. He keeps an eye on the place during the night. He'll be patrolling the halls after you go to bed for the evening."

Hugh nodded to them.

"Now," said Hal, "does anyone have any questions before we begin?"

Lubek stepped forward. "I have a question for Hugh."

"Yes?" Hal prompted.

Lubek frowned. "This question is for *Hugh*."

"And I'm *listening*," Hal replied patiently. "What *is* it?"

"I want Hugh to answer my question!" Lubek said through clenched teeth.

"How can I *answer* it," Hal replied, now with equally clenched teeth, "if you don't *ask* it?"

"Gahhh!" Lubek pushed past Hal, grabbed Hugh by the arm, and started speaking to him in a low voice.

Natasha nudged Oleg. "What do you think Lubek is talking to Hugh about?"

"He's not talking to me," Oleg whispered back. "He's talking to the security guy."

Natasha looked at him for a moment and then sidled toward the pair to eavesdrop on their conversation.

"Tell me," Lubek was saying, "what should

my students and I do if the electricity fails again?"

"It won't," Hugh replied stiffly. "The backup generator has taken over."

"But what if *that* quits?"

Hugh crossed his arms over his massive chest. "The only way that would happen is if someone deliberately turns it off. And no one would do that!"

"Why not?"

"Because then anything that needs electricity won't work. I'm talking lights, elevators, security systems, you name it, it'll be powerless. Even" —Hugh's voice turned ominous— "*the vending machines!*"

Lightning flared again and a clap of thunder shook the roof.

"Well," Hal called suddenly, "shall we begin?"

He led the group into a small theater.

Natasha motioned for Oleg to sit next to her. She quietly filled him in on what she had overheard. "Oleg, we've got to keep Lubek from shutting down the generator!"

"Right!" Oleg replied, making a defiant fist. "We can't lose power to the vending

machines!"

Natasha rolled her eyes. "No, we can't lose power to the museum's security systems! If we do, then Lubek will be free to steal anything he wants!"

Chapter Four

Age Before Beauty

Once she was sure Oleg understood the problem, she outlined a solution. "I'll continue to shadow Lubek. First chance you get, sneak away, find the generator, and stand guard, okay?"

Oleg nodded. "You can count on me."

Further planning was cut short because Maya plunked next to them. Then Hal called for their attention.

"I need a volunteer who'd be willing to have

their picture shown on this screen." He gestured toward a wall-sized monitor behind him.

Kelly stood up immediately. "I'll do it!"

"Kelly wants to see herself on a big-screen TV? What a shock," Maya muttered.

Hal trained a camera on Kelly and a moment later, her face filled the screen.

"You see before you the image of a lovely young girl," Hal said.

Kelly simpered. The image simpered, too.

"But watch what happens when we add twenty years to her age!" Hal turned a dial a few clicks. Wrinkles appeared around Kelly's eyes and mouth.

"Hey!" Kelly cried. The image mouthed an outraged "Hey!"

"Then forty years." A few more clicks and the skin under Kelly's eyes and chin sagged.

Her blond hair thinned and turned ashy with gray. "Then sixty! Or how about *eighty*?"

Kelly shrieked. Her face morphed into an openmouthed death mask.

"Whoops! Sorry!" Hal hurriedly clicked off the program.

Kelly stumbled over to Greg. "I need a hug!"

Greg looked from the screen to Kelly and back. "Um, maybe later," he mumbled, clearly not interested in kissing a girl who a moment earlier had looked like a corpse.

"'Maybe *later*?'" Kelly went from needy to furious in point two seconds. She yanked the gold-and-diamond bracelet from her wrist and thrust it into his hand. Then she covered her eyes dramatically. "Maybe *not*! You can have this back! I don't ever want to see it or you again!"

"Whatever." Greg dropped the bracelet into his pocket as Kelly stormed off.

"This way, please!" Hal ushered them into another room filled with computers, pulled back a chair in front of a terminal, and held up a thin wire. "If I could have a volunteer?"

Everyone looked at Kelly.

"You've got to be kidding," she said.

"I'll do it." Natasha came forward and sat in the chair.

"Excellent!" Humming happily, Hal fixed one end of the wire to her forehead and plugged the other end into another, smaller computer. "This electrode will pick up on changes

your body experiences while viewing the image on this screen." He tapped the large terminal and then turned on the small computer. A thin line scrolled across the smaller monitor. "This is your current body status. Any changes will register here."

He told her to study the photo on the bigger screen. "Can you tell me what's wrong with it?"

Natasha examined the picture. "It's just a messy bedroom. I don't see—AUGH!"

For one fleeting second, the messy bedroom had disappeared, replaced by an extreme close-up of Kelly's shrieking death  mask. The gruesome face had only flashed there for  a moment before the bedroom reappeared, but that brief vision had shaken her enough to make the line on the small computer jump wildly.

"Okay," she said, pulling the wire from her head and standing up. "I am officially creeped out. Next!"

Natasha was helping Maya put the wire on when she heard Lubek and Hal arguing. "Sir, I really must insist that you stay with your students," Hal was saying.

"I was just looking for Hugh," Lubek replied huffily.

"But I have been here the whole time!"

"Gahh!"

"Be right back," Natasha said to Maya. She edged over to Oleg, leaned down, and pretended to tie her shoe.

"Psst, Oleg," she whispered. "I think Lubek was getting ready to make a move on the generator! You've got to get there first and guard it! Do you need me to make a distraction so

you can get away?"

Oleg didn't reply.

"Oleg?" She straightened up and looked around.

Oleg had disappeared.

Chapter Five

Now Hear This

"Hey, did you see where Oleg went?" Natasha asked Maya.

Maya shrugged. "I don't know. Bathroom, maybe? Why?"

"Oh, no reason." Natasha smiled to herself. *Bathroom, right! He's on his way to the generator.* She spotted Lubek pacing in the hall. *That leaves Zoravian Enemy Number One for me to stick to like paste!*

"I've seen all I need to see here," Lubek was

telling Hal impatiently. "Can we please move on?"

"Fine, fine," Hal replied. He led them to an enormous glass dome.

"Ladies and gentlemen," he said theatrically, "you are about to experience"—he unlocked the door to the dome with a swipe of a key card—"*sound*!"

"I don't hear anything," Greg complained loudly as he filed into the room. *Thing—thing—thing* . . . His voice echoed off the walls. Greg looked delighted. "Hey, cool!"

Cool—cool—cool . . . came the echo.

"Shhhh!" Hal's shushing whispered around the dome like the hissing of snakes. He picked up a guitar and in a loud voice began to lecture. "Now then, a quick lesson about sound. Sound is made by vibrations. The more intense the vibration"—he strummed the guitar lightly, then with more and more force until the noise level was deafening— "the louder the sound. Right? Okay. Moving on."

He put down the guitar. "When sound vibrations reach our eardrums, we hear noise. But we are not capable of hearing all noises. Some are simply too faint. Of course, there are ways to make such noises louder."

He picked up an object from a nearby table and showed it to them.

"That looks like the microphone that came with my karaoke machine," Maya whispered to Natasha.

"To the untrained eye," Hal said, "this may look like a microphone that comes with a typical

karaoke machine—"

"Told you!" Maya muttered.

"—but it is actually the most sensitive amplifying device in the world!" Hal pulled a matchbox from his pocket and opened it. "*Behold*!"

The class leaned forward and beheld.

"It's . . . an ant," Maya said.

"Precisely!" Hal fit a metallic cone over one end of the amplifier and placed the open end of the cone over the box. "Now silence, please! And listen!"

He flicked a switch on the amplifier. Suddenly, a noise like hail bouncing on a tin roof filled the room. Natasha and the others clapped their hands to their ears. Hal clicked off the microphone.

"Told you it was sensitive," he said smugly. "You just heard an ant's footsteps."

He lifted the cone from the table, brushed the ant to the floor, and pocketed the match-box. Then he opened the bottom of the amplifier and pulled out a flat round object.

"Looks like a video-game disk," Maya whispered.

"To the untrained eye, this may look like a video-game disk, but it is actually a sophisticated storage device. With it, we can record, replay, and analyze inaudible sounds at our leisure." He reinserted the disk and pressed a button. The ant's footsteps reverberated around the dome again. He switched off the machine, leaving the room in complete silence.

The silence didn't last long, though. An enormous crack of thunder pounded overhead, shaking the dome's walls.

Hal chuckled. "Good thing we didn't amplify that!" He patted the microphone. "Thunder caught by this baby would be the equivalent of a sonic boom. Vibrations from a sonic boom are so intense they can shatter glass." He gestured to the glass dome. "If we'd heard it, we'd be covered in millions of razor-sharp glass splinters right now!"

"Such vibrations could also topple buildings, bring down bridges, even destroy palaces, couldn't they?" Lubek's eyes were shining with evil glee. "Why, whole cities could be, shall we say, 'thunderstruck,' should such a device fall into the wrong hands!"

33

Natasha's blood turned cold. She knew exactly whose hands he wanted the amplifier to fall into—*his!*

Chapter Six

Lights Out . . . Again

"Er, yes, I suppose such destruction would be possible," Hal answered Lubek. "But we have taken every precaution to be sure such a theft can't happen." He held up the key card. "This room locks automatically and can only be unlocked with this. And of course the dome is protected in other ways. It—"

"Quiet!"

Hugh stormed into the room. He shot Hal a fierce look and then turned to the class. "It's late. Time for you all to get settled for the night. Girls will be in the east wing, boys in the west. Hal," he added with a growl, "you come with me."

"Uh-oh, I think someone's in trouble!" Maya said to Natasha. "Come on, let's get our stuff!"

Natasha kept a careful eye on Lubek as she filed out. He was standing outside the dome, the same evil smile on his face. That smile faded, however, as Hal left and the door locked tight after him.

"Natasha, you coming?" Maya called.

"Yeah!" Natasha replied. She hurried to join Maya, but not before observing Lubek rap the

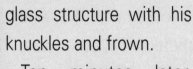

glass structure with his knuckles and frown.

Ten minutes later, Natasha and Maya were in the bathroom getting ready for bed. Suddenly, a scream pierced the night.

Natasha and Maya exchanged a look. "Kelly," they said together.

They found her shaking Greg by the shoulders violently. "You *lost* it?"

Greg broke free from her grasp and searched his pockets. "I guess it fell out."

Lubek appeared then, looking disgruntled. "What is the problem here?"

Kelly stabbed a finger at Greg. "He lost my diamond bracelet!"

"You said you didn't want to see it ever again anyway!" Greg pointed out.

"You know I didn't mean that!" She shoved Greg to the ground.

"A diamond, you say?" Lubek cut in. "And it's

here in the museum somewhere?"

Kelly gave a huff of annoyance. "Yes!"

"Well, then," Lubek said, looking thoughtful, "it must be found!"

Greg started to get up. "Fine. I'll go look—"

Lubek shoved him back down. "No! I shall

search for the bracelet! After all, a diamond is a very valuable object and should not be trusted with just anybody. The rest of you, get to bed!"

Kelly gave Greg one last push and then stormed off toward the east wing. Greg stumbled off to the west wing. Lubek headed into the main museum hall.

Natasha took a step after him but Maya

pulled her back. "Where are you going?" her friend said. "Our beds are this way!"

Natasha didn't want to let Lubek out of her sight, but she had no choice but to follow Maya back to the east wing. A few minutes later, she was zippering herself into her sleeping bag alongside the other girls.

"Well, see you in the morning!" she said.

 She rolled over and waited for her classmates to fall asleep.

And waited. It seemed like hours until the other girls finally stopped chatting. When it had been silent for a while, Natasha lifted her head. "Psst, Maya, are you asleep?"

"Mmmbphlmph," Maya mumbled.

"I'll take that as a 'yes.'"

Natasha slipped out of her bag. She quietly

unzipped her backpack and took out her spy suit, utility belt, and super-powered glasses. Then she stuffed her backpack into her sleeping bag to make it look like she was still inside. She hurried to the rest room, changed into her spy gear, and tiptoed into the main hall.

Suddenly, there was a loud *zap*—and for the second time that night, she was plunged into total darkness. This time, however, there had been no flash of lightning. Something else had zapped the power.

Oh, no! she thought. *Lubek!*

Chapter Seven

A Diamond is Lubek's Best Friend

Natasha switched her glasses to night vision and broke into a run, heading straight for the glass dome. She was worried about Oleg— *Lubek must have over-powered him in order to get to the generator*—but knew she had to keep her

SOUND DOME

enemy from stealing the amplifier before she could help her friend.

When she reached the dome, she breathed a sigh of relief. The door to the exhibit was still closed. Lubek wasn't in there after all!

Then a movement inside the room caught her eye. She gasped. Lubek *was* inside! But how?

Then she saw it. Near the door handle was a hole. On the floor inside the exhibit was a cir-

cle of glass. And hanging from Lubek's pocket was Kelly's bracelet.

I don't believe it! she thought. *There really is a diamond in that bracelet!* She figured that Lubek must have found the missing jewelry, used the diamond to cut a hole in the glass, and then reached through to open the door from the inside.

And now he's *inside. Of course, that doesn't mean he's going to get out again!*

She tiptoed up to the door, snaked her hand through the hole, and worked the handle. The door swung open silently. She slipped inside and carefully closed it again.

"*You!*"

Natasha whirled around.

Lubek stood at the far side of the room, glaring at her. The amplifier was next to him.

Natasha got into fighting stance, fists at the ready. "Yes, me," she retorted. "I'm here to

stop you from stealing that amplifier!"

Lubek gave a soft laugh. "I don't think so." He picked up Hal's guitar and charged her, swinging the instrument like a bat. The strings whistled as they cut the air.

Natasha darted for cover behind a large table littered with beakers and tubes. Lubek swept the table clean with the guitar. Natasha threw up her arms to protect herself from the flying shards.

Over the tinkling of broken glass, she heard a rumble of

thunder followed by a crow of delight. She looked up to see a nasty, triumphant smile spread across Lubek's face.

"Excellent!" he said. "My chance for revenge on the people of Zoravia has come! Once I have the amplifier, I will capture the loudest clap of thunder I can and use it to topple King Carl's precious kingdom!" He threw back his head and laughed. "Thunderstruck! Everything in Zoravia will be thunderstruck!"

"Not if I can help it!" Natasha grabbed the edge of the table and slid feet first beneath it.

Her momentum propelled her right into Lubek's left leg.

Wham!

"Owwww!" Lubek's howls of pain echoed around the dome.

Natasha swung back up to her feet. One eye on the amplifier and the other on Lubek, she flipped the table on its edge and vaulted over it.

"Keee-aai!" Her boots thudded into his stomach.

"Ooof!" He dou-bled over.

"Eeee-ya!" She leapfrogged over his back—grabbing Kelly's bracelet as she

passed—and ran to the amplifier. She stretched out her hand and had almost grabbed it when *twang!* A long wire with a tiny, three-pronged hook at the end snaked through the air and wrapped itself tight around the device's handle. Then it retracted, taking the amplifier with it. She twisted around to see the device fly across the room and into Lubek's waiting hands.

"What is that, a cheap knock-off of Spider-Man's web-slinging powers?" she taunted.

"Why, you—" Lubek's angry reply was cut short when a new sound echoed through the room. The sound was a soft whirring like machinery powering up.

The generator's coming back online! she realized. Lubek must have decided the same thing. He stuck the amplifier into his belt and bolted out the door.

Natasha started after him. Suddenly the room was flooded with red light and she found herself caught in the midst of hundreds of crisscrossed security beams.

Chapter Eight

Beam Me Out!

Natasha stood frozen in place. *If I break one of these beams, I'll set off an alarm. If I set off an alarm, Hal and Hugh will find me here. If Hal and Hugh find me here, they'll discover Kelly's bracelet in my pocket. They'll think I'm a thief and detain me in their office! And worst of all, Lubek will get away!*

She groaned. *This is bad.*

She shifted her gaze right and left, trying to see if there was another exit nearby. Nothing.

Right. Looks like it's limbo time!

She took a few quick breaths to steady herself. Then she slowly bent backward and slipped her head and shoulders beneath the closest beam. When her upper body was through she straightened up and eased one leg, then the other, over the next beam.

Two down! Only twenty more to go.

Sweat began to bead on her forehead. She wiped it away and began to move through the next set of beams. She was balanced on one leg, the left side of her body halfway through, when a drop of perspiration rolled down to the tip of her nose.

Oh, no. She willed the drop to stay put as she

shimmied the rest of the way over the beams. Just as her right foot touched the floor, the drop let go. She caught it a split second before it fell through a beam.

That was a little too close!

Five painstakingly slow minutes later, she had finally reached the door. *Now to find Lubek!*

There was just one problem. She had no idea where Lubek had gone.

She ran into the hall and looked around in desperation. Her gaze fell on a staircase that led to the balcony above the main exhibit hall.

Maybe I'll be able to spot him from up there!

"Nnnnn-aaaaaah!"

She stopped dead, her hand on the railing.

Probably just the wind. She started up the stairs.

"Nnnnnn-aaaaaah!"

Not the wind!

She looked around, trying to find whatever was making the noise. But the place was empty.

Okay, so the museum is haunted by some weird disembodied voice at night, she thought. *Nothing to be afraid of!*

The moan came again.

Yeah, right!

She sprinted up the stairs and raced across the balcony. At the end was a ladder up to a small hatch in the roof. Natasha hesitated.

"Nnnnnnn-aaaaaaaah!" came the moan from below.

She grabbed the bottom rung, climbed to the hatch door, and pushed it open. She hauled herself through and landed with a flop on top of the museum's rain-soaked roof.

"Come on, come on, come on," she heard a sinister voice say. She raised her head. Lubek was on the other side of the roof, holding the  amplifier aloft. She could see that its power light was on.

I've got to get it before it thunders again!

She got into a crouch and began sneaking toward him. Halfway there, a bolt of lightning streaked across the sky. In the sudden light, Lubek spotted her.

"You! *Again!*" he bellowed.

She got into a crouch, ready for the attack. He set the amplifier down and charged her.

"You won't stop me this time!" he cried as he hurled himself at her.

"Wanna bet?" She jumped straight up, pressed the antigravitational button on her elbow pad, and somersaulted over his head.

"Hey!" He flew past her, grasping air, and landed face first in a puddle.

She landed on her feet next to the amplifier.

Twang!

Once more, Lubek sent his wrist wire zinging toward his prize. This time, however, Natasha was ready. She grabbed the small hook with one hand, the length of wire with the other, and pulled. Hard.

"Whoa!" Lubek slid across the slick roof like a penguin tobogganing on the ice. Natasha quickly looped the wire around a nearby pole, threaded it through the hook, and clamped the hook in place—just as Lubek sailed off the side into the air.

Twang! Thud! "Ooof!"

The wire pulled tight and snapped Lubek back into the building. Natasha listened to his angry threats for a moment, and then picked up the amplifier, tucked it into her utility belt, and headed back into the museum.

Chapter Nine

Night, All!

"I'm telling you, someone is creeping around this museum! I saw a figure on the security cameras!"

Natasha was halfway down the ladder when she heard the voices. She froze.

"When did you last check on the kids?" Hugh asked.

"When the power came back on. They're all in bed."

"What about the teacher?"

Silence.

"I thought he was with you," Hal said finally.

"Do you see him here with me?" Hugh made an exasperated sound. "What is with you? First you almost give away our security secrets and now you lose track of the group's leader! Sheesh!"

"Why don't we just split up and look for him?" Hal said. "He's got to be hanging around here somewhere."

Oh, he is! Natasha thought of Lubek swinging from the wire and suppressed a laugh.

Grumbling, Hal took off toward the east wing. Hugh muttered something under his breath and then hurried off in the opposite direction.

When she was sure he was gone, she crept the rest of the way down the ladder, turned, and ran right into Oleg.

"Princess! What are you *doing* here?" he gasped.

"I was waiting for Hugh to leave!" she said.

"Leave? I didn't think you knew I was here!"

"No, I meant . . . oh, never mind. I'm just glad to see you're all right!" Then she frowned in puzzlement. "Hold on, you *are* all right! How come? Didn't Lubek overpower you at the generator?"

Oleg looked sheepish. "Um, actually, Lubek

got to the generator before I did. I was temporarily delayed. Stuck, you might say."

"Stuck? Where?" Oleg didn't answer.

Natasha looked at him closely. "What's that white stuff around your mouth?"

He hung his head.

"Oleg, did you find some paste and eat it?"

He pulled a small jar from his lab-coat pocket and looked at it sadly. "I thought it was paste anyway. Turns out it was some kind of super-sealant disguised as paste. My lips stuck together."

She thought of the weird moaning she'd

heard. "You tried to call me when your mouth was sealed, didn't you?" she guessed.

He nodded. "The generator is near the security office. There are monitors there. When I saw Lubek go to the roof, I got on the intercom and tried to warn you!"

She almost told him how his moaning had scared her to death. But instead, she said, "We've got to return the amplifier to the dome and get back to our sleeping bags before we're missed!"

Luckily, they managed to make it to the sound exhibit undetected.

"It's kind of a mess, isn't it?" Oleg whispered, peering at the hole in the wall, the turned-over table, the broken guitar, and the shattered glassware.

"Yeah, but what can we do?" Natasha said glumly.

Oleg was silent for a moment. "I have an idea." He whispered his plan to her.

"Oleg, you're a genius! You want me to help?"

He shook his head. "You've had enough adventure for one night."

She gave him her super-powered glasses and the amplifier. "Good luck, then!"

As he slipped into the room to navigate the security beams, she started back to her sleeping bag. Midway across the dark hall, she came to a large window. The thunderstorm had ended at last and the full moon was peeking out from behind the lingering clouds.

Lubek suddenly swung past, legs flailing. Somehow, he managed to plant his feet against the window. He gripped the wire and began climbing up the building, hand over hand. Then he glanced inside. His eyes locked on hers.

She sucked in her breath and, stepping backward, melted into the shadows.

Chapter Ten

Clear Skies Again

"Hey! Wake up, sleepyhead!"

"Mmmmm?" Natasha rolled over in her sleeping bag, sat up, and stretched. "Is it morning already?"

"Sure is!" Maya said. "You sleep like a rock, you know that? I looked over at you at one point last night and it was like you weren't even *breathing*!"

Natasha glanced at her backpack and hid a smile. Fifteen minutes later they were in the cafeteria with the other students. Lubek stumbled in soon after. He had dark circles under his eyes and his shirt was on inside out. The students took one look at him and moved to the other side of the room.

Natasha spotted Oleg by the cereal station and hurried over to him. "How'd everything go after I left?" she murmured as she picked up a bowl.

Oleg produced the jar of supersealant. It was

 empty. "This stuff is truly amazing! It repaired all the broken glassware and fixed the hole in the dome so cleanly even I can't tell anything was ever wrong!"

They stopped talking then because Kelly walked by, in deep discussion with Hugh. Kelly broke away and headed across the room.

"Mr. Lubek!" she called.

Lubek was sitting alone at a table, gripping a cup of hot coffee. When Kelly approached he snarled, "I did not sleep well and do not wish to be disturbed."

She put her hands on her hips. "I just want to know if you suc-  ceeded in getting what you went out to get last night. Because if you did- n't, Hugh will get it."

Lubek rose slowly and leaned across the table. "Are you *threatening* me?" he asked dangerously.

Natasha hurried over, and with a deft sleight of hand, she slipped Kelly's bracelet into his

 pocket. "Uh, Mr. Lubek? I think Kelly is talking about her bracelet."

"Oh." Lubek took out the bracelet and tossed it to Kelly. "There. And be more careful with your things next time!" He sat back down and hunched over his coffee.

Kelly rushed across the room to where Greg was standing and threw her arms around him.

"Guess everything's back to normal now," Oleg said.

"Yeah," Natasha agreed. "By the way, where did you put my, um, special eyewear?"

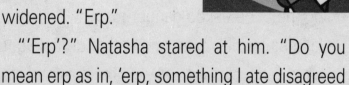

"Your—?" Oleg's eyes widened. "Erp."

"'Erp'?" Natasha stared at him. "Do you mean erp as in, 'erp, something I ate disagreed with me'? Or 'erp, I forgot them in the dome'?"

Just then, Hal came waltzing into the cafeteria. He was whistling loudly—and wearing Natasha's spy glasses.

"Who is making that confounded *noise*?" Lubek growled. He started to lift his head.

"Oleg," Natasha whispered urgently, "we've got to get those before Lubek sees them!"

"Right!" Without a further word, Oleg tackled Hal and threw him to the ground. The glasses flew off the old man's face and landed in a box of cereal. "Um, sorry, but your whistling was disturbing my teacher."

In a flash, Natasha grabbed the box and shook it over her bowl. The spy glasses fell out along with the cereal.

"Hey, cool toy!" Maya said. "And the box isn't even specially marked or anything!"

"Pretty amazing!" Natasha said. She winked at Oleg and quickly slipped the specs into her backpack. "In fact, my good luck has me completely thunderstruck!"